Hello Herky!

Aimee Aryal

Illustrated by Julie Reynolds

MASCOT BOOKS

www.mascotbooks.com

It was a beautiful fall day at the
University of Iowa.

Herky was on his way to Kinnick Stadium to watch a football game.

He walked to the Main Library.

A professor passing by said,
"Hello Herky!"

Herky stopped at
Iowa Memorial Union.

A group of students standing outside
waved, "Hello Herky!"

Herky walked over to
Danforth Chapel.

A couple walking by said,
"Hello Herky!"

Herky stopped at
Carver-Hawkeye Arena where the
Hawkeyes play basketball.

He ran into Coach Alford there.
The coach said, "See you
next basketball season Herky!"

It was almost time for the football game.
As Herky walked to the stadium,
he passed by some alumni.

The alumni remembered Herky from
when they went to the University of Iowa.
They said, "Hello, again, Herky!"

Finally, Herky arrived at the stadium.

As he ran onto the football field,
the crowd cheered, "Go Hawks!"

Herky watched the game from the
sidelines and cheered for the team.

The Hawkeyes scored six points!
The quarterback shouted,
"Touchdown Herky!"

At half-time the Hawkeye Marching Band performed on the field.

Herky and the crowd sang
the "Iowa Fight Song."

The Iowa Hawkeyes won
the football game!

Herky gave Coach Ferentz
a high-five. The coach said,
"Great game Herky!"

After the football game, Herky was tired.
It had been a long day at the
University of Iowa.

He walked home and climbed into bed.

"Goodnight Herky."

For Anna and Maya,
and all of Herky's little fans. ~ AA

To all the University of Iowa students who have
portrayed Herky over the years and to the Mills and Reynolds families;
especially my Nephew Alder and my Niece Annika. ~ JR

Special thanks to:

Steve Alford

Dale Arens

Kirk Ferentz

Christa Roberts

For information please contact Mascot Books,
P.O. Box 220157, Chantilly, VA 20153-0157.

IOWA, UNIVERSITY OF IOWA, HAWKEYES and HERKY are trademarks or
registered trademarks of the University of Iowa and are used under license.

ISBN: 1-932888-05-5

Printed in the United States.

www.mascotbooks.com